For the children of Eldorado
where we all love the rain.

Will Hubbius

Mendel's

LADDER

Mendel's LADDER

By
Mark Karlins

Illustrated by
Elaine Greenstein

SIMON & SCHUSTER
BOOKS FOR YOUNG READERS

Mendel Moscowitz was seven the summer it didn't rain. Day after day the grown-ups listened anxiously to the weather report, and the children peered at the sky, looking for signs of rain. At night, when Mendel's father filled the tub, the water ran slowly. And in Mendel's backyard the flowers and vegetables he had planted wilted and drooped.

On the sixty-first rainless day, a Wednesday, Mendel knelt down and started to work. He hammered together a wooden crate, the side of a baby's crib, a screen door, three bent bicycle wheels, and all the other junk he had gathered from around the neighborhood.

His mother, a cello teacher by trade, halted her lesson and leaned out the window. "Mendel, what's with all the noise?"

"I'm working," said Mendel.

"With scraps of wood, you're working? With rubbish?"

"I'm building a ladder," Mendel called, "to the clouds."

At that moment Mrs. Effie Studge, the neighborhood gossip, was listening by her window. She flung a kerchief over her curlers, grabbed her shopping cart, and ran out the door.

At Feld's butcher shop, after bargaining over a chicken, Mrs. Studge talked. "Flo's son, Mendel, you know him? Wait till you hear what crazy shenanigans he's up to now. Mendel," she started to laugh, "he's building a ladder . . . to the clouds!"

The news spread fast. Before long everyone in Flatbush was laughing and whispering.

The big kids shouted at him as they ran past, "Mendel, are you ever a loony!"

A group of grandmothers playing a game of canasta on a nearby fire escape shook their heads and tssked. "You're a foolish boy, Mendel."

The girls in front of his building chanted in time to their jump rope, "Mendel, Mendel, such a schmendrel."

Mendel didn't like the teasing. But he shut his ears to it and kept building.

By the end of the week the ladder was done. Mendel began to climb.

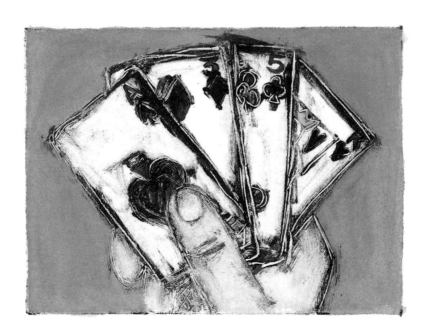

Mendel's mother, stirring soup, glanced out the window. Seeing Mendel, she dropped the spoon and ran down the fire escape. "Mendel, come back!" she yelled.

Mendel's father, who had been working on his stamp collection and snacking on some sesame seed candy, shoved the bag in his pocket and came running after. "Mendel, you get off that ladder right now!" he shouted. "There'll be no climbing to the clouds today, young man!"

Mendel climbed faster. "I have to find the Rainmaker," he called back.

His parents stood horrified at the bottom of the ladder. What could have gotten into their Mendel's head? But crazy or not, Mendel was their one and only child. They gripped the sides of the ladder and climbed up after him.

Mrs. Studge leaned out the window. "Wait till the neighbors hear about this," she cackled as she grabbed for the phone.

It was a long climb. After heaving themselves onto the cloud, Mendel and his parents collapsed in a sweaty clump.

"I don't like what you're doing, Mendel," his father said. He leaned back on one elbow. "But this cloud . . . not so bad, very soft."

"Why, Mendel? Why?" his mother moaned.

"I have to find the Rainmaker," said Mendel, and he stood up and once again began his search. "My garden needs water."

His parents groaned to their feet and followed.

The Rainmaker, one Maxwell Butterbarrel, lounged in a sagging overstuffed chair, holding a newspaper in front of him. He was still in his bathrobe. On either side of him newspapers and coffee cups were piled high.

"So," said Max, peering at them over the top of his paper, "you came all the way up here maybe for some reason?"

"My garden needs rain," explained Mendel.

"If you don't mind, I'm reading," Max replied as he rustled his paper.

Even Mendel's mother was interested now. "All of New York needs rain," she said.

"Not to mention New Jersey," added Mendel's father, reaching into his pocket for a sesame seed candy.

"Please, I'm not so interested in your problems. I've got my own," Max said. He eyed the sesame seed candy. "Besides, it's a little late to ask."

"Too late?" they wondered out loud. "Why?"

"Why? I'll tell you why. No one appreciates, that's why. Way back when, a long, long time ago, people knew what to do. They made prayers, gracious thank-you's, offerings—a bit of corn, a goat. But now not a single 'please,' not a single 'thank you,' not a single 'my, what a good job you've done,' 'what a splendid rain that was.'"

"I *love* the rain," said Mendel softly.

"Complaints, that's all we get," Max continued, ignoring Mendel and eyeing the new sesame seed candy Mendel's father was unwrapping. "'It ruined my picnic.' 'I can't play outside.' 'I can't go to the beach.' I'm telling you, it's enough to make anyone discouraged. So what we did, all the Rainmakers, we decided: no offerings, no work. That's that. Period."

"I appreciate you," said Mendel.

"It's easy to say," huffed Max.

Mendel noticed Max again eyeing his father's candy. He thought for a moment and then looked hard at his father. His father stared back. "So, Mendel, what's with you?" Mendel moved closer and whispered in his ear.

Mendel's father then took two big steps toward Max. He bowed his head and extended both arms. Cupped in both hands was a pile of sesame seed candy, the cellophane wrappers glistening in the sun.

Max's face glowed with delight. "Now, that's what I call an offering!" he said, and unwrapped one of the candies.

Twelve candies later, Max heaved himself out of his chair, pulled out four sparkler wheels from his bathrobe pocket, and handed three to Mendel and his parents. "You'll need these," he said.

"Sparkler wheels!" Mendel exclaimed, holding a round, flat wheel by its stem. "But what are we supposed to do with them?"

Max grinned and shoved the stem up and down. Sparks flew out. "You'll see," he said.

Then, opening the tall doors of the cabinet that stood next to his chair, Max declared, "Grab those wings. It's time to make thunder!"

Mendel and his parents pulled out the huge wings. Dusty, a bit tattered, each wing was a hodgepodge of feathers Max had collected from molting birds that had passed through his cloud—pigeons, sparrows, crows, ducks, and even a flamingo that had escaped from the Bronx Zoo. And there was more besides. The wings were decorated with things the wind had grabbed from below—hats, balloons, kites, laundry pulled off the line, a black toupee.

Brushing off the dust, the three strapped on the huge feathered wings.

Max flapped. Up he went.

Mendel flapped. Up he went.

Mr. and Mrs. Moscowitz flapped. Up they went.

They circled, they swooped, they looped the loop.

"Look at me!" called Mendel. He flew upside down. He flew with both eyes closed, his legs crossed. He flew high and did a backward midair somersault!

"Enough already!" commanded Max, beckoning them to him. Mendel and his parents flew over to Max and hovered, awaiting instructions. Max puffed up his chest. "Follow me!" he barked, and then as they approached a large cloud, he ordered them: "Now spin your sparkler wheels!" They did. Sparks flew. Lightning bolted.

"Good," said Max. "Now, pump those wings. Harder! Harder! Harder!"

They did, and from their wings boomed great waves of thunder.

The clouds shook, shimmied, huffed in and out, until the rain came spattering down.

It rained on New Jersey. It rained on New York. It rained on Mendel's backyard.

Mendel and his parents made a soft landing on Max's cloud. They returned the wings to him. "Thank you," they said.

"It's been a pleasure," said Max.

"Here," said Mendel's father, taking the bag from his pocket. "You keep these candies. They're for you."

"Thanks," said Max, flapping his wings as if again ready for flight.

Mendel and his mother and father began climbing back down the ladder. There below was the whole neighborhood, crowded in their backyard. An old man had taken off his hat so the rain could patter on his bald spot. A baby was catching raindrops in her mouth. Even Mrs. Studge, who had grabbed one of her geraniums and was holding it up to the rain, looked happy.

And Mendel's garden? His vegetables looked perky, his flowers lifted their leaves to the rain.

Mrs. Studge looked up. "It's Mendel!" she called. "Hurray for Mendel!" Mendel held on to the ladder with one hand and waved.

And high above them all was Max and the sound of distant thunder.

For Jacob,
Rebus mutatis credite
——M.K.

For Isaac
——E.G.

SIMON & SCHUSTER BOOKS FOR YOUNG READERS
An imprint of Simon & Schuster Children's Publishing Division
1230 Avenue of the Americas, New York, New York 10020
SIMON & SCHUSTER BOOKS for YOUNG READERS
is a trademark of Simon & Schuster. Book design by Paul Zakris.
The text for this book is set in 13-point Stone Informal.
The illustrations are monoprints.
Manufactured in the United States of America
10 9 8 7 6 5 4 3 2 1

Library of Congress Cataloging-in-Publication Data
Karlins, Mark.
Mendel's ladder / by Mark Karlins ;
illustrated by Elaine Greenstein.
p. cm.
Summary: One summer during a drought, Mendel builds
a ladder to the clouds and sets out to find the Rainmaker.
[1. Droughts—Fiction. 2. Rain and rainfall—Fiction.]
I. Greenstein, Elaine, ill. II. Title.
PZ7.K14245Me 1995 [E]—dc20   94-6838 CIP AC
ISBN: 0-671-89726-8